Princess Swashbuckle

For Sam, Nathan and Charlotte – H.H.

For Isabel, love – D.A.

BLOOMSBURY CHILDREN'S BOOKS
Bloomsbury Publishing Plc
50 Bedford Square, London, WC1B 3DP, UK

BLOOMSBURY, BLOOMSBURY CHILDREN'S BOOKS and the Diana logo are trademarks of Bloomsbury Publishing Plc

First published in Great Britain by Bloomsbury Publishing Plc

A catalogue record for this book is available from the British Library

ISBN 978 1 4088 6280 3 (HB)
ISBN 978 1 4088 6281 0 (PB)
ISBN 978 1 4088 6279 7 (eBook)

1 3 5 7 9 10 8 6 4 2

Printed and bound in China by C & C Offset Printing Co Ltd, Shenzhen, Guangdong

All papers used by Bloomsbury Publishing Plc are natural, recyclable products
from wood grown in well managed forests. The manufacturing processes
conform to the environmental regulations of the country of origin.

To find out more about our authors and books visit www.bloomsbury.com and sign up for our newsletters

Princess Swashbuckle

Hollie Hughes
&
Deborah Allwright

BLOOMSBURY
CHILDREN'S BOOKS

LONDON OXFORD NEW YORK NEW DELHI SYDNEY

Once upon a time
in a faraway land and place,
there lived a frog princess
with a green and slimy face.

THE GRAND FROG BALL

Swashbuckle was her name
and she had a lifelong dream,
to one day rule the waves
as a froggy pirate queen.

But . . .

Her mum and dad weren't happy,
"A pirate's life won't do!
We need to find a handsome prince –
the **perfect** one for you."

"How about young Hubert?
He's a fine and handsome frog."
"No way," wailed Princess Swashbuckle.
"He lives beside a bog."

"Make a match with Gerald then –
now *there's* a clever frog!"
"No, thank you," said the princess.
"He lives beneath a log."

"Well, settle down with Jasper
in his charming, neat abode."
"You're joking!" spluttered Swashbuckle.
"He's actually a toad!"

Swashbuckle thought about her life
in Frogland with her prince,
and realised quite quickly,
"There's more to me than this!"

So she packed up all her things
and decided to set sail.
Then **jumped** aboard a pirate ship
and herein lies her tale . . .

The pirates of the Stinky Fish
were sadder than could be –
their captain had swum back to shore
and left them all at sea.

It was clear to Princess Swashbuckle
they needed someone new.
And, deep down in her froggy heart,
she knew what she had to do.

"Now,
listen up,
you barnacles!
I'm Captain
of this crew,
and we're going
on a mission
to find NICE
things to do."

"Hip, hip hooray!" the pirates cheered.
"At last we've found our way."

"Quick! Climb the rigging, sweep the decks,
heave ho – anchors aweigh!"

So Pirate Captain Swashbuckle
took everything in her stride,
and sailed off with her Stinky Crew,
helping creatures far and wide.

They helped a wandering whale to find a **home** inside a cave . . .

They helped a quiet, timid mouse learn how to be more **brave** . . .

They helped a snake to bake a cake
and start a cooking school
(and every pirate tum agreed
that helping folk was cool!).

News of the Stinky's kindly deeds
spread over land and sea . . .

and every day was happy
for the pirate family.

Until . . .

One day, Princess Swashbuckle felt funny in her tummy.
She knew she must be homesick,
for she missed her dad and mummy.

So she sent a gift to Frogland
of a never-empty spoon,
a pot of laughs,
a pile of smiles,
and cheesecake from the moon!

It seemed that sending love back home
helped to make things better,
as then, one day, by parrot post,
there came a golden letter . . .

We're sorry Swash,
wrote Mum and Dad.
You didn't **need** a prince.
We rue the day
you went away,
we've missed you ever since.
We love you and we wish you
forever near and dear.
Please **come back** to Frogland
and have adventures here.

Mum & Dad

Straightaway the Pirate Captain
knew exactly what to do.
She asked the wandering whale for help
and waved 'bye to her crew.

The King and Queen
awoke next day
and got the
BEST surprise . . .

their darling
Princess Swashbuckle
right before
their eyes!

So the King and Queen retired and
Queen Swashbuckle took charge.

She ruled the waves a pirate queen
aboard the royal barge.

The years ahead were action-packed . . .

with voyages . . .

fun . . .

and laughter.

And everyone in Frogland
lived happily ever after!